Phil and Lil Go to the Doctor

by Becky Gold
illustrated by Robert Roper

SIMON SPOTLIGHT
An imprint of Simon & Schuster Children's Publishing Division
New York   London   Toronto   Sydney   Singapore
1230 Avenue of the Americas, New York, New York 10020

KLASKY
CSUPO INC.

Based on the TV series Rugrats® created by Arlene Klasky, Gabor Csupo, and Paul Germain as seen on Nickelodeon®

"We gots band-its!" Phil and Lil shouted as they ran into Tommy's backyard.

"I fell down and got an owwee," Phil told Tommy and Chuckie.

"No, *I* fell down and got an owwee," Lil said. "You're a copycat, Philip."

"Am not, Lillian!"

"Prove it! Take off your band-it," Lil told him.

"No! Mommy said we gots to keep 'em on," said Phil.

"Is your owwee bleeding?" Chuckie asked Lil.

Lil nodded and peeled off her bandage. "Ouch! That hurts!" Then she proudly showed everyone the scab on her knee.

"Blood!" Chuckie yelled, and ran to hide.

Just then Tommy's mom, Didi, came outside with Phil and Lil's mom, Betty.

"Did you talk to the twins about their checkup tomorrow?" Didi asked. "Dr. Lipschitz says it's good to let little ones know what to expect at a doctor's office."

"Oh, that Dr. Lipschitz could take the adventure out of any childhood," Betty replied. "But in this case, Deed, he's probably right. I'll prep the pups."

"Did you hear that, Lil?" Phil asked.
Lil nodded. "What's a checkup?" she wondered.
Phil shrugged. "I dunno."

Soon Susie and Angelica came over. "What's up, guys?" Susie called out.

Chuckie peeked out from the bushes. He saw that Lil had put the bandage back on her knee. With a sigh of relief, he joined his friends.

"Mommy's taking us for a checkup," Lil told Susie. "Do you know what that is?"

"Sure," Susie said. "My mom's a doctor. I know all about checkups. The doctor checks to make sure that you're healthy. She takes your temperature and finds out how much you weigh. She looks down your throat and in your ears and stuff."

"Why, Susie?" Phil asked.

"To see if you have a bug," Susie told him. "People bring lotsa bugs to the doctor's office!"

"Wow!" Phil and Lil exclaimed. Checkups sounded great!

Then Angelica said, "If the doctor finds a bug, she'll give you a rooster shot."

"It really doesn't hurt very much," Susie assured the twins.

"Oh, yes it does!" said Angelica. "It feels just like this." She pinched the twins' arms.

"Ow!" shouted Phil and Lil.

"You're a meanie, Angelica!" Tommy cried.

"Aw, I was just showing them what a doctor does," said Angelica.

"Don't worry," Susie told the twins. "Doctors are very nice. They even give you treats to take home."

"Get lotsa extras!" Angelica said.

The next morning Betty put Phil and Lil in their car seats. "Time for your checkups," she told them. "It's gonna be a snap—and Dr. Kiddair's a sweetheart."

When they got to Dr. Kiddair's office, he was busy. They waited in the waiting room.

"Do you see any bugs?" Phil asked Lil.

"Not yet," said Lil.

Phil and Lil were a little afraid when Dr. Kiddair asked them to come into his office with their mommy.

"Would you like to sit up high?" he asked the twins, gently lifting them up.

Phil and Lil smiled. The bench felt soft.

Betty helped Phil and Lil take off all their clothes except their diapers.

"Maybe he'll check our belly buttons," Phil whispered to Lil.

"Yeah, and find something good and nummy," Lil whispered back.

DOCTOR'S REPORT
NAME Lillian DeVille
NAME Philip DeVil

"First let's take your temperature with this thermometer," said Dr. Kiddair. "This will tickle a little bit."

The twins giggled as Dr. Kiddair put the tip of the thermometer inside their ears. It did tickle!

"Very good," Dr. Kiddair said. "Your temperatures are normal."

"Okay, Phil," said the doctor, "I need you to stick out your tongue really far. Say 'ahhhh'!"

Phil and Lil giggled. Phil stuck out his tongue and said, "Ahhhh!" Dr. Kiddair pressed on it gently with a wooden Popsicle stick. He shined a special flashlight into Phil's mouth. Then he did the same with Lil.

"Your throats look fine," Dr. Kiddair said.

"Now I'll use an otoscope to look in your ears," said Dr. Kiddair. "Hmm . . . no cabbages," he joked.

The twins' eyes grew wide. They had found lots of good stuff in their ears before, but never cabbages!

Then the doctor brought out his stethoscope and listened to their hearts.

"Your heartbeats are strong and even," he told them.

"You two are great patients," said Dr. Kiddair.

"I'm proud of you, pups," Betty agreed. She looked at her watch. "Oops! Be right back—I need to feed the meter."

As Betty left the room, the phone rang. Dr. Kiddair picked it up.

"C'mon, Phil," Lil whispered to her twin. "I know there gots to be bugs around here somewhere!"

"It's time for your booster shots," Dr. Kiddair told them. But the phone rang again, and he picked it up.

"I don't want that shot," Phil whispered to Lil.

"Me neither. Let's hide!" said Lil.

"Did you see your twins anywhere?" Dr. Kiddair asked Betty when she returned. "I'm afraid the babies are missing!"

Betty laughed. "Oh, they're somewhere, I'm sure." She picked up two lollipops that lay on the counter. "Lollipops! Come and get 'em!" she said.

Lil peeked out from behind the plant. Phil poked his head out of the closet.

The twins came out of their hiding places and got their lollies. Betty scooped them up for a hug.

A few seconds later Dr. Kiddair said, "All done!" Their shots were so quick, they didn't even know they were getting them!

What's more, the doctor put some colorful bandages on their arms!

"I still wish we coulda got a bug," Lil whispered to Phil.

On the way home Phil spotted something in Lil's hair. "Look!" he said, picking out a ladybug. "We did get a bug after all!"

Lil grinned. "You know what, Phil? I can't wait for our next checkup!"